P9-DNZ-495

Oh, A-Hunting We Will Go

John Langstaff

Oh, A-Hunting We Will Go

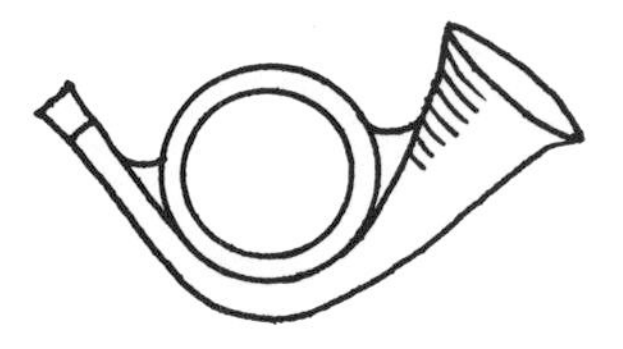

pictures by

Nancy Winslow Parker

A Margaret K. McElderry Book

Atheneum 1974 New York

Library of Congress catalog card number 74-76274

ISBN *0-689-50007-6*

Published simultaneously in Canada by

McClelland & Stewart, Ltd.

Manufactured in the United States of America

Printed by Connecticut Printers, Inc., Hartford

Bound by A. Horowitz & Son/Bookbinders

First Edition

For all the children
who helped me make up extra
verses for this folk song.

U.S.
Oh, a-hunting we will go,
A-hunting we will go;
We'll catch a fox

And put him in a box,
And then we'll let him go!

Oh, a-hunting we will go,
  A-hunting we will go;
We'll catch a lamb

And put him in a pram,
And then we'll let him go!

Oh, a-hunting we will go,
A-hunting we will go;
We'll catch a goat

And put him in a boat,
  And then we'll let him go!

Oh, a-hunting we will go,
A-hunting we will go;
We'll catch a bear

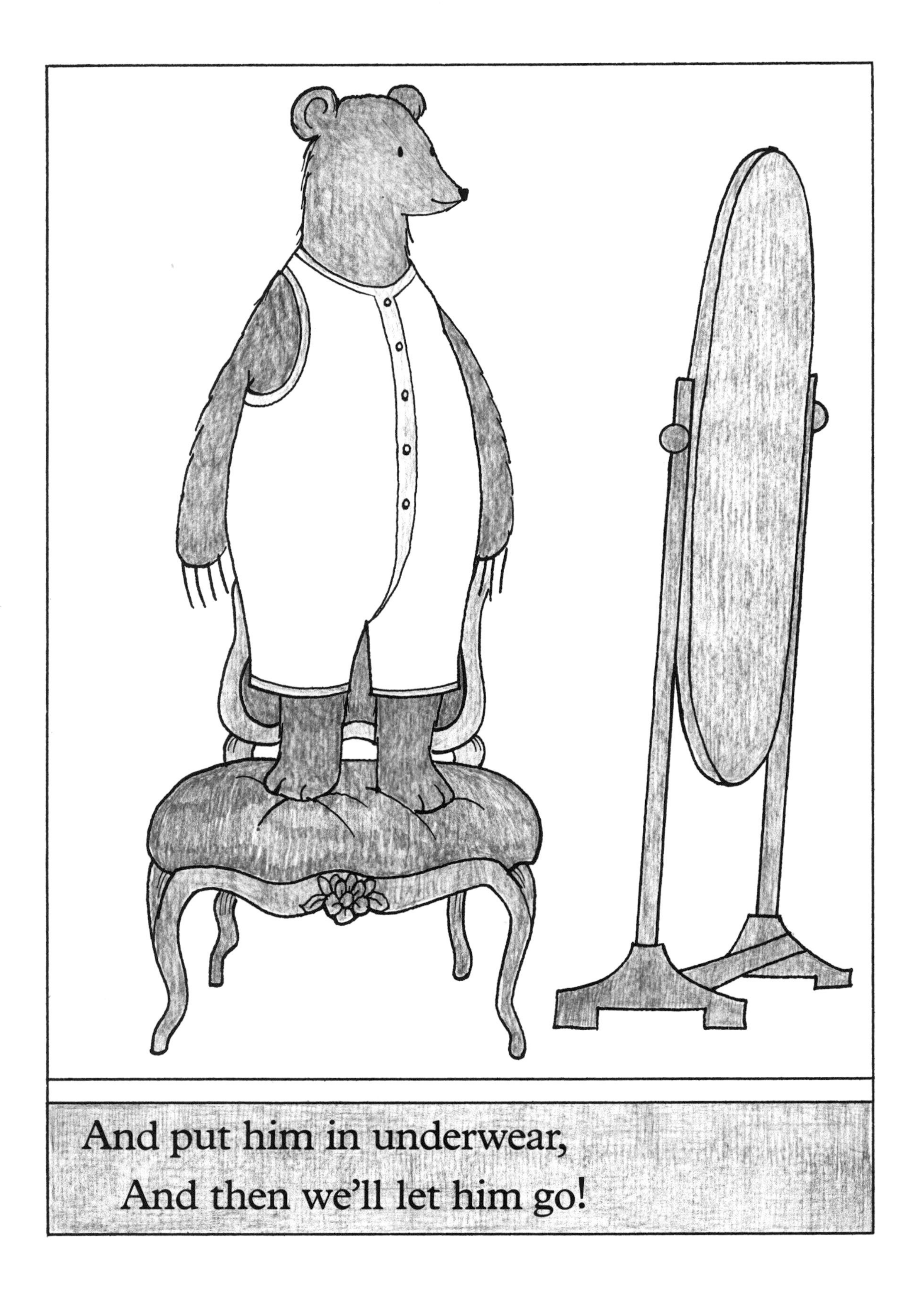

And put him in underwear,
And then we'll let him go!

Oh, a-hunting we will go,
  A-hunting we will go;
We'll catch a whale

And put him in a pail,
And then we'll let him go!

Oh, a-hunting we will go,
  A-hunting we will go;
We'll catch a snake

And put him in a cake,
  And then we'll let him go!

Oh, a-hunting we will go,
A-hunting we will go;
We'll catch a mouse

And put him in a house,
And then we'll let him go!

Oh, a-hunting we will go,
A-hunting we will go;
We'll catch a pig

And put him in a wig,
And then we'll let him go!

Oh, a-hunting we will go,
A-hunting we will go;
We'll catch a skunk

And put him in a bunk,
And then we'll let him go!

Oh, a-hunting we will go,
A-hunting we will go;
We'll catch an armadillo

And put him in a pillow,
And then we'll let him go!

Oh, a-hunting we will go,
A-hunting we will go;
We'll catch a fish

And put him in a dish,
And then we'll let him go!

Oh, a-hunting we will go,
A-hunting we will go;
We'll catch a brontosaurus

And put him in a chorus,
And then we'll let him go!

Oh, a-hunting we will go,
  A-hunting we will go;
We'll just pretend and in the end,
  We'll always let them go!

Oh, A-Hunting We Will Go

We'll catch a lamb and put him in a pram,
And then we'll let him go!

We'll catch a goat and put him in a boat,
And then we'll let him go!

We'll catch a bear and put him in underwear
And then we'll let him go!

We'll catch a whale and put him in a pail,
And then we'll let him go!

We'll catch a snake and put him in a cake,
And then we'll let him go!

We'll catch a mouse and put him in a house,
And then we'll let him go!

We'll catch a pig and put him in a wig,
And then we'll let him go!

We'll catch a skunk and put him in a bunk,
And then we'll let him go!

We'll catch an armadillo and put him in a pillow,
And then we'll let him go!

We'll catch a fish and put him in a dish,
And then we'll let him go!

We'll catch a brontosaurus and put him in a chorus,
And then we'll let him go!

We'll just pretend and in the end,
We'll always let them go!